Filmstrip

CHIPOLLINO

By Book
Gianni Rodari

ISBN: 9781792683770

Chipollino "in Italian means" onion ". The hero of the book is the writer Gianni Rodari and was a boy-onion. And all the inhabitants of the country, which is told in a fairy tale, were akin to some fruit or vegetables. In Chipollino, instead of curly hair on his head, tufts of green onions stuck out. He was perky and funny, hated injustice, boldly stood up for his friends and was not afraid of offenders.

You will learn about the adventures of an onion-boy when you watch this filmstrip.

Here he is, Chipollino, son of Chipollone. Together with his parents
and seven brothers, he lived on the poorest suburb.

Once their places were visited by the ruler of the country Prince
Lemon himself.

The whole street ran to look at the prince. Chipollone and
Chipollino were in the front row. They were pressed back so hard
that Chipollone could not stand the onslaught

and inadvertently stepped on the leg of Prince Lemon.

Oh! -Lawned Lemon. - It's a riot! Grab a villain!

Goodbye, Chipollino! -Chipollone shouted in despair. "Now you have no one to hope for and only life itself will teach you to the mind"

And Chipollino decided to go traveling to learn from the life of the mind.

Soon on the way he came across a small village. Her first house was so tiny that it was impossible to call him even a house. In it sat an old man, whose name was Pumpkin.

Pumpkin just the day before he finished building his house. All his life he dreamed about him and every year he bought brick by brick. He worked a lot, but the bricks were added slowly, and of them it was still impossible to build a house. So years went by. Finally, the day came when Pumpkin felt that he was getting old. "We must start the construction", he decided. His house turned out so cramped that the Pumpkin could only live in it sitting.

Barely Chipollino and Pumpkin had time to meet, when suddenly a carriage approached the house. A fat man came out of it, puffing and puffing ... It was Signor Tomato, the ruler of the rich landowners Countess Cherries.

"Robber!", shouted Signor Tomato. "You built a house on the land of Countess Cherries. Get out of here right now so that you burst!"

-Even earlier you will burst, Signore Tomato! These bold words were spoken by none other than Chipollino. Signore Tomato turned red with anger

and clutched his hair. And suddenly ... tears splashed out of the Signor Tomato's eyes. The reason for these tears was the onion hair of Chipollino.

The Tomato was cruel and heartless to a man; nothing could squeeze tears from his eyes. - "Sneaky boy, ragged, you will pay me dearly for these tears!"

To escape the shame, signor Tomato jumped into the carriage.
However, fleeing, he shouted to the Lemons, who came with him:
"Immediately throw the Pumpkin out of the house and plant the
most evil dog in it".

Lemon without much talk kicked the Pumpkin out of the house, and
instead they brought a hefty dog named Mastino.

11

All these events took place on a hot summer day. Mastino, left to guard the possessions of Countess Cherries, was exhausted from thirst. Chipollino saw it. "Now I'll play a joke with him!" He thought.

He poured water into a bottle, poured sleep powder in there and pretended to drink. Poor Mastino was so thirsty! "Signor Chipollino, let me sip a sip?"

-You are welcome. Drink as you like. - The dog greedily drained the bottle to the bottom ...

Immediately he fell and fell asleep.

Seeing that the terrible dog was sleeping, the villagers began to converge to the house of the Pumpkin godfather. They were really scared: "Signor Tomato twice stayed out in the cold. He will not forgive us."

"I know what to do," said Chipollino. - We have to hide the house. It can be easily transported on a trolley in a secluded place.

14

And the next day, Chipollino, together with the girl, whose name was Radish, took the domino of the Pumpkin godfather to the forest to his friend, the godfather Blueberry.

Signor Tomato immediately reported the disappearance of the house. He immediately sent a detachment of police to the village.

Lemons have arrested everyone who has fallen under their hand - the godfather Pumpkin, Professor Pear, Leek ...

Chipollino and Radish, not finding anyone in the village, immediately guessed what was the matter. Chipollino decided to help the captives by all means, and they went to the castle of the Countess Cherries to reconnoiter.

The castle stood on top of a hill. He was surrounded by a huge park. There were a lot of ads in the park,

and they were all written for the nephew of the Countess Cherries, poor Cherry orphan. Cherry forbade everything and even play with village children. And now he wanders alone in the park.

-Signor Cherry! - he suddenly heard. Cherry turned around and saw a boy that looked like an onion, and next to him was a girl, whose pigtail had a radish tail just like the tail.

Cherry was so boring to one that he, forgetting the ban, approached him. The guys quickly met. Chipollino told them one funny story, and soon they were laughing so merrily that ...

... their laughter flew to the castle. Such ringing laughter here have not heard. - What is it? - worried Countess Cherries.

and sent the Knight of the Tomato to find out what was the matter.

What did he see ?! Cherry in a friendly conversation with two ragged !!! Moreover, in one of them Signor Tomato recognized Chipollino!

The Tomato has gone berserk. "Well, scoundrel," he croaked, "I'll put you in a special chamber." Simple prison is unworthy of you! "

and Chipollino was thrown into the darkest chamber.

But it turned out that another creature lived in the chamber - it was
the Mole. He chose this dark chamber, because it suited him more
than others for habitation: after all, moles are seen only in
darkness.

21

Mole and Chipollino met. "Would you like to dig a move to some dark place?" Suggested the Mole. One plan immediately flashed near Chipollino.

He thought about the dungeon, where the Pumpkin, the Pear, and others were languishing. "I think we should dig to the right," he said to Mole. "Right, to the right, I don't care."

When they were very close to the cell where Chipollino's friends were sitting, he revealed his secret to the Mole. - "So they need to be released? Well, I agree. "

The Mole took up the job again and soon pierced the dungeon wall. But, unfortunately, at this very moment, the Bow Leek lit a match. The Mole clutched at his eyes and disappeared into the darkness.

And Chipollino rushed into the arms of his friends. How delighted
the prisoners were!

Meanwhile, the quiet and timid Cherry was determined to free his
new friend. In the whole house only one person loved him - the
servant Strawberry. With it, Cherry developed a plan of action.

Cherry found out from one of the Lemon that Tomato holds the
keys to the prison in stockings.

Late at night, when Tomato was fast asleep and he had pleasant
dreams, Cherry and Strawberry sneaked into his bedroom and
pulled the keys out of the stocking.

25

Further events unfolded as follows: Strawberry began to call for
help in order to divert the prison guard,

and Cherry rushed to the dungeon.

The joy of all prisoners was indescribable. - "Hush, my friends," Cherry warned them. "We must run until the guards return."

When Lemon ran to the prison, they did not find anyone there.

Do you know who Mr. Carrot is? Famous specialist in tracing.
Simply put, detective. He and his dog Derby-Grab were invited by
Signor Tomato to find the escaped prisoners.

Mr. Carrot began by pulling out the cube number 28 from some
bag. This meant that he had to step aside 28 steps and look for
fugitives there.

He and his dog took 28 steps and ... got into the pool.

"I came to a brilliant conclusion," Carrot said without
embarrassment. - The fugitives dug an underground passage in the
pool. - But Signor Tomato did not agree with this and ordered the
detective to send a search on a less complicated path.

29

Then the famous detective and his dog went to the forest.They walked peacefully through the forest, developing a plan of action as they went along. all of a sudden happened to them something strange ...-

Carrots and Hold-Grab rapidly soared up!

This idea came up with Cherry. He had read adventure books and knew all the hunting tricks. Two enemies were permanently disabled.

В ЗАМКЕ ГРАФИНЬ ВИШЕН БЕСПОРЯДКИ СОБЛАГОВОЛИТЕ ПРИСЛАТЬ БАТАЛЬОН ЛИМОНЧИКОВ ЖЕЛАТЕЛЬНО ПРИСУТСТВИЕ ВАШЕГО ВЫСОЧЕСТВА КАВАЛЕР ПОМИДОР

Without receiving any news from Mr. Carrot, Tomato decided to act on his own. He sent a telegram to Prince Lemon.

The next morning, Prince Lemon arrived at the castle of the
Countess Cherries, accompanied by the court Lemons and the
whole battalion of Lemon.

The Counts Cherries were ordered to get into the carriage and go
along with His Highness to search for the fugitives.

The castle is empty. Then Cherry, through a secret passage, led Chipollino and everyone else hiding nearby. The enemy fortress was occupied by friends.

The night has come. Prince Lemon ordered to break in the woods camp and arrange fireworks. Fireworks he was special. Shooting from a cannon with soldiers seemed to him a very funny sight.

Signor Tomato was terribly agitated: to grind as many soldiers on missiles, what a folly! To calm his nerves, he went for a walk. And suddenly he saw that the windows of the castle they had left behind were lit up!

Signor Tomato immediately rushed into the forest and told the prince terrible news.

A strategic plan was developed. Prince Limon ordered all officers and soldiers to smear their faces with black paint in order to frighten the besieged.

The first to attack the castle went to the squad, consisting of forty select generals. The "heroic" detachment approached the foot of the hill on which the castle stood.

35

The besieged were preparing for protection.

When a squad of Lemons was going up the hill, a projectile rushed
from the hill. He attacked the generals and began to crush them.
So the tower of the Countess Cherry's castle served Chipollino and
his friends well.

In the storerooms of the castle, Chipollino and Cherry found a whole battery of wine bottles. And when Prince Lemon launched a new attack, they attacked the attackers very kindly - they doused them with intoxicating liquid,

The Lemons were drunk to insensitivity and at once, as if on cue, lay down on the ground and snored.

The reign reigned in the castle!

But our friends didn't have long to rejoice: from the capital for
reinforcement a whole division of Lemons arrived to the prince.

The castle was taken.

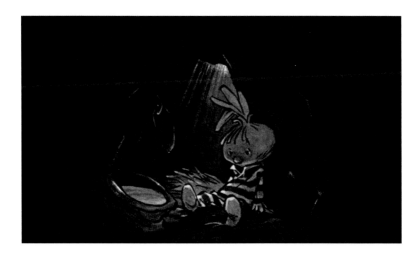

Cherry as a punishment locked in the attic. And Chipollino and his
friends, of course, were sent to prison again. The onion-boy was
planted in an underground chamber. It was even darker than the
one where he had been sitting before.

The yard was round. The prisoners walked in a circle one by one. It was strictly forbidden to talk.

Suddenly, in one of the prisoners, Chipollino recognized his father. - "Father!" - "Chipollino, my boy!" - Father and son, crying, embraced.

And then a shout followed: "Hey! You two! March ahead! "- Old
Chipollone broke away from his son and took his place. After this,
the walk seemed to them even more dismal.

-"Chipollino!"-"who is calling me?"-"underpass is ready. You only
need to jump a step to the right, and the Earth collapses you have
under your feet. " "Mole! -realized Chipollino. -He remembers me!
He helped me! "

-Pass it around the circle, whispered Chipollino running ahead,
striking an arrestee to this site each did step right and jumped.
There's an underground passage.

And went. With every crawl someone hopped the right and
vanished without a trace.

Warden looked worriedly at the prisoners. "Why they became less?" it was considered, but every time it flounders. Then it became to look at the sky – not flown off anyone from prisoners.

At this point, the rest disappeared underground, and not left in the prison yard.

At a time when the prisoners made their way to underground move, police rounded up all the inhabitants to the foot of the highest hill, where was decorated with flags of the dais.

From this dais, Prince Lemon deigned to read to his subjects a new decree he had just published.

The prisoners quickly moved through the underground passage, made by the Mole. Only the Pumpkin, whose huge head was stuck in a narrow passage, lagged behind.

The Decree, which read Prince Lemon stated that because Prince is the owner of the land and air in his country, he establishes a tax on deposits.

"So-so!" Quiet!" said Chipollino. - I think this is the voice of the prince. - The prisoners have quieted down.

"I dug my way to the very platform," said the Mole. Get out one by one. Nobody will see you under the platform! And I will help the Pumpkin: he seems to be stuck again.

Carefully breaking a hole under the platform, Chipollino climbed out himself and helped the others out.

The prince finished reading the edict and looked around menacingly at the silent crowd.

47

... Finally, in the hole of the underground passage, the bald spot of the Pumpkin appeared. He tried in vain to squeeze through a narrow hole.

The Mole, wanting to help him out, swung his shovel,

and pumpkin bomb flew out of the underground passage! With his crown he gave way to the platform so much that he flew up into the air along with everyone who was on it!

Prince Lemon and his retinue, rattling sabers and orders, rolled down so quickly that no one had ever seen them after that. They said that they went abroad.

The chain of police was broken. The crowd surged towards the
captives, and the banner of Liberty soared above the high hill.

The noise and joyful cries of the people reached the castle.
Grabbing a telescope, Signor Tomato ran four steps down to the
highest tower.

And what did he see! A jubilant crowd led by the damned
Chipollino, whom he had twice imprisoned, was approaching the
castle.

What is it? Ah, everything is clear: this is Signor Tomato burst in
anger! Well, that is where he is dear.

Now the castle is no longer a castle, but the Palace of Children. There is a drawing room, a puppet theater, a cinema, and many different games.

And most importantly – there is a school. Chipollino and Cherry sit at the same desk and teach arithmetic, grammar, and various other things that you need to know in order to defend against cheats and oppressors and keep them away from their country.

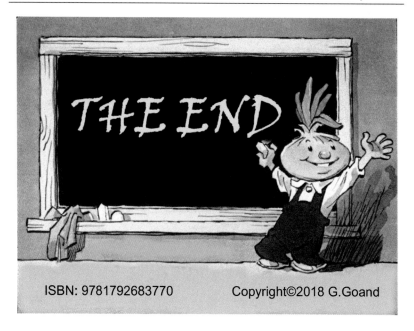

ISBN: 9781792683770   Copyright©2018 G.Goand

Made in the USA
Monee, IL
22 December 2020

55112657R00033